FOR HONOUR AND NOT FOR GLORY

DAVID BRETT SAUNDERS

Books by David Brett Saunders

ROMANS & BRITONS
For Honour And Not For Glory

VIKINGS & SAXONS
All Sins Must Be Paid For

LATER MIDDLE AGES
Cast No Shadow

HIGH MIDDLE AGES
Awful The Many Foul Deeds

Copyright © 2021 David Brett Saunders

Designed by Jeremy Paxton

Set in 11pt Palatino Linotype

Printed in the UK

All rights reserved

1 4 6 8 10 12 14 16 18

ISBN: 978-0-9567753-4-4

No part of this publication may be reproduced, stored in a retrieval system, or in any form or by any means, without the prior permission in writing of the author, nor be otherwise circulated in any form of binding or cover other than that in which it is published and without a similar condition including this condition being imposed on the subsequent publisher.

List of Contents

Dedications 2

A Literary Quote 3

List of Tribes, Place Names & Characters 4

List of Roman Legions & Roman Characters 5

Statement 6

Story Chapters 1 to 23 7

Epilogue 65

*Dedicated to my wife Bev
and my lovely daughters
Emma, Claire and Amy*

*Also dedicated to Tristan Marshall-Luck
who inspired the name of my main character*

*And in fond remembrance of all the
wonderful books of Rosemary Sutcliff*

A Literary Quote

*"What is honour? A word.
What is in that word honour?
What is that honour? Air.
A trim reckoning!
Who hath it?"*

Part of Falstaff's "Honour Speech" soliloquy
in Act V, Scene One, of Henry IV Part 1
written by William Shakespeare (1564-1616)

List of Tribes, Place Names and Characters

TRINOVANTES
Tribal centre: Camulodunon = Roman colonia of Camulodunum = now Colchester, Essex = tribal capital of Trinovantes and later taken over by Catuvellauni and with fictional characters = **Drustan** and **Silla**

CATUVELLAUNI
Tribal centre: Verlamion = Roman municipium of Verulamium = now St. Albans, Hertfordshire
King Cunobelin – **Epaticcus**, his brother – **Togodumnus**, eldest son – **Caratacus**, middle son – **Adminius**, youngest son

ATREBATES
Tribal centre: Calleva = Roman town of Calleva Atrebatum = now Silchester, Hampshire
King Verica and **Bericus**, his son = fictional character

ICENI
Based in Norfolk and parts of Suffolk and Cambridgeshire
King Prasutagus – **Queen Boudica** and her two daughters

CANTIACI in Kent
CORIELTAUVI in East Midlands
BRIGANTES in Yorkshire
SILURES in South East Wales

Other Place Names
Londinium = London
Ratae = Ratae Corieltauvi = Leicester
Mona = Isle of Anglesey, North West Wales
Gesoriacum = Boulogne-sur-Mer, France
Durocortorum = Reims, France
Tamesis = River Thames
Oceanus Britannicus = English Channel

List of Roman Legions and Roman Characters

2nd Legio II Augusta
9th Legio IX Hispana
14th Legio XIV Gemina Martia Victrix
20th Legio XX Valeria Victrix

Emperor Claudius (reigned AD41-54)

Emperor Nero (reigned AD54-68)

Aulus Plautius = Commander of Roman army in AD43 invasion and Governor of Britannia AD43-47

Vespasian = Commander of Legio II in AD43 invasion and later Emperor (reigned AD69-79)

Gnaeus Hosidius Geta = Commander of Legio IX in AD43 invasion

Publius Ostorius Scapula = Governor of Britannia AD47-52

Gaius Suetonius Paulinus = Governor of Britannia AD58-60

Quintus Petillius Cerialis = Commander of Legio IX in AD60 revolt and much later Governor of Britannia AD71-73

and fictional characters from a turma of Legio XX
= a troop of cavalrymen attached to a legion –
Frontinus, **Didius**, **Marcus** and **Galbus**
and also **Dracus the troop commander**

Statement

A man can have many names and a man can show many faces to the world. A man can do good things and do bad things, and sometimes he can do things he never thought he would ever allow himself to do.

At times if you listen to people you may agree with everything they say, admit that everything they tell you is right, and then decide to do precisely what you think and that be totally wrong.

And what you think you know isn't always important.

You may see many places and visit countries and peoples you had never even heard of, but your old homeland has a powerful hold on you that will eventually pull you back......

Chapter 1

He ran and he ran and he ran; falling over tree roots, slipping in the mud and stumbling in rabbit holes……

He had been a fool to get into a fight with Adminius over the girl Silla - but he liked her - and thought that she liked him too. They had been friendly for most of their fourteen or fifteen years since childhood in the village; though he had never really had the occasion to take things further with her.

But since the Catuvellauni tribe had taken power over them things had changed for their Trinovantes tribe. It seemed whatever the leaders of the Catuvellauni wanted they got and the three sons of King Cunobelin were the worst.

His youngest son Adminius, a cocky and spoiled brat, had taken an interest in young Silla; she was attractive and fiery in equal measures and she had gained an avid admirer in Adminius.

But Drustan had reacted to his attempted assault on her virtue and got into a fight with him that had led to bloody noses and might have moved on to the drawing of daggers but Cunobelin's other sons, Togodumnus and Caratacus, were also in the dun that day meeting the village elders.

They came over and pulled them apart and broke up the fight; they roughly threw Drustan to the ground and then punched and kicked him.

"Boy, you'd better not mess about with us" said Togodumnus, "we rule here now and you'd better not forget it."

One of the village hounds growled at the Catuvellauni warriors and bared its teeth; Caratacus kicked out at the dog who slunk away.

"You are even worse than the rest of your tribe as I hear your mother is a whelp of the Atrebates, and we will be taking over their lands soon too."

At this insult to his mother Drustan dragged himself up and flung his dagger at Caratacus; he just missed and Caratacus' eyes flashed wide and brutally.

"Now it is time to teach you some more about the power of the Catuvellauni and who rules here. Tie him to that wagon wheel over there and we will lash the skin off his insolent back."

But before they could grab him he slipped out of the grasp of the other warriors and ran towards the village entrance, evaded the guards on the gate and made it out into the nearby margins of the forest outside.

The undergrowth quickly thickened and Drustan kept running; he had been in the forest round here many times, tracking and hunting animals, but now that he was being chased it felt slightly more unfamiliar and slightly more intimidating.

The sounds of the pursuit were getting nearer but he could not hear the baying of any hounds following his scent - it had all happened too quickly for them to organise a proper chase.

Gradually as he went deeper into the woods he found that he knew some of the old tracks and pushing on he could hear the noise of those following lessen.

After more time he knew he was quite far away from the dun. He had no food, no water and no dagger; he was tired, thirsty and hungry and he didn't really know what to do now.

He found a small green, brackish pond in amongst the trees and slaked his thirst - it tasted awful and was barely drinkable but it was so badly needed.

What should he do? He knew Cunobelin's sons and warriors were only supposed to be visiting the village that day, so could he try and go back or would they have left instructions for him to be held?

Chapter 2

It started to rain and he was soon soaked through; he pulled his old cloak round him as best he could and decided to head back towards the village to see how things looked. He could at least try and see what was happening from the edge of the forest.

He was nearing the dun when suddenly he was grabbed and forced to the ground. He tried to get up but a heavy man sat on him and held him down.

"You make too much noise, boy" said a dark bearded man who he knew to be an old friend of his father. "You always were a wild one! Aiee, but you remind me of your dead father so; he could not take a slight either. Your mother is beside herself with worry. You cannot come back as the men of the village have been told to hold and chain you up and send you off to Verlamion for punishment at the pleasure of the King's sons."

"Have you come to capture me then?" asked Drustan.

"No, you young fool, by my faith to your father I have come to help you, if that is possible to manage with you being such a hot-head."

The old man got off him and stood up. Drustan could just see that there were flecks of grey in his beard and there were deep wrinkles in his weathered face.

"Your mother says you must go and try and find any of her remaining relatives in the South with the Atrebates. She had an older brother called Kenan who might still be alive in the tribal centre of Calleva who you could try to go to. It is not safe to stay here."

He took off his shoulder a large, old leather bag.

"Here is some food for you from your mother - bread, cheese, apples and a flask of sweet mead."

"Please thank her - I'm starving!"

"Best ration it out sparingly though."

"Tell her I love her too and will miss her."

"And from me I give you an old but sharp dagger and a sword that belonged to your father. I have kept it a long time waiting for you to grow up and now there is no time left but this. Use it with valour to the honour of your family but do not debase it with over-weaning false pride."

"I will do my best to bring honour to my father and my mother."

"Now be off with you and try to steer clear of trouble. Head to the South towards the great river Tamesis and go to your right along it to cross at one of the distant fords or somehow find a boat to take you across it. Then carry on until you reach the lands of the Atrebates, but be careful as some is now held by the warriors of the Catuvellauni."

"How will I know my uncle?"

"Your uncle will know you with your black hair and daft expression I am sure" chuckled the old man. "So now you must be away with the early dawn light and I must sneak back in by the midden pit saying I have been out for a piss before I am missed for the day ahead. May our gods protect you, for I am sure you will have many hard times ahead of you. Farewell Drustan."

And with that he slipped away through the trees, growing ever more indistinct in the early morning mist.

"Goodbye" Drustan called after him quietly.

Drustan put the bag over his shoulder, put the dagger in his belt and then picked up his father's old sword. He felt scared about the future away from the only home he had ever known, but he felt proud to be holding his father's sword and hoped he would learn to use it well.

So he turned to go and headed off through the dense undergrowth towards what he judged was the South West veering away from the rising sun. He had a long way to go.

Chapter 3

Drustan kept moving at an angle to the sun and found a large clump of trees to sleep in the next night. He ate a little food and drank some mead. A light rain fell but he took shelter in the lee of the roots of a blown down old tree.

The next morning the sun came out slightly sickly looking. Drustan carried on and eventually reached what he guessed must be the big river Tamesis – it was wide and he wondered how he would ever get across.

There were no people about so he started walking to the right keeping away from the bankside and any open spaces. Finally he came to the edge of a small village; several dogs barked and he pulled back into the fringes of the nearby forest.

He kept a lookout and saw that by the riverside there was a little rickety wooden jetty with a couple of canoes tied up. The boats were thus just outside the boundary fence of the village and he wondered if they stayed there overnight he might be able to get hold of one to use to cross the river.

It looked deep and the current seemed quite fast-flowing and he hadn't got much experience of boats so he felt a bit uneasy. However he had to somehow get across that water – it was as simple as that if he wanted to reach the Atrebates.

He saw a strange old man with a white beard wearing a cloak covered in bird feathers. An old brindled dog lolloped along beside him as they headed down to the jetty.

The dog stopped and growled at the bushes near where Drustan was hiding. The old man looked over too but shook his head slowly.

"Maybe you can smell rabbits old girl, but I don't want you running off chasing them now – come on let's get in the canoe and go fishing."

Now Drustan had been thinking that maybe he could overpower that old man but the dog would make an awful noise and surely attract the attention of others in the village.

Whilst he was thinking all this he was moving quietly through the undergrowth, and then he tripped up over a tree root and landed with a thump that knocked the breath out of him.

Suddenly the old man appeared above him brandishing a wooden stick.

"Who are you and what are you doing here, boy?"

His dog growled a bit but didn't make any other movement towards him.

Drustan pulled himself upright and looked over at the old man – even though he had that big stick he didn't really look too menacing.

"Well I am out travelling to go and see some kin. They are a long way over there beyond the great river and I was just thinking and wondering how to cross. Perhaps you could maybe help by taking me over?"

"Why should I do that and what for! If you don't know how to get across why do you come so sneakily? Surely you would want to see our village elders and seek their help and assistance."

"No, no, I was just trying to avoid any bother. I saw you getting ready to go out in a canoe and I just wanted to catch up with you – I mean no harm and I only want to get to the other side over there. Surely you could please help me as I am alone and very tired you know."

"You ask a lot for no reward to me."

"Well I could help you row across and also give you a drink of mead from my flask."

"Now you're talking; I am partial to a good mead – it is good is it?"

"Very fine, my mother helped make it."

"Well then maybe I'll reconsider. What do you think dog?" said the old man. The dog wagged its tail now and also seemed more relaxed.

"Right I'll help to take you across, but you'll have to do some of the work. I certainly could do with a hand as I'm not as young as I was and I have no family left since the last sickness."

So they went together down to the jetty and piled into one of the wooden canoes. He cast off and they paddled away from the riverbank. The current caught them and pushed them out into the middle of the river; they had to dig in and paddle hard to make progress.

The old man turned and eyed him slightly suspiciously.

"Where are you from and why were you trying to avoid getting too near to the village?"

"As I said I am just trying to reach the other side to be with some kinfolk over there. I've never met them and have never been this far away from home. I have left my mother and I feel sad about that."

"Bet you're running away from something."

"Maybe I am but I am not out to cause you any trouble."

"Alright then; you seem fair enough for a youngster to me, so let's crack on. We've got a way to go yet."

They paddled on and the old man skilfully negotiated the swirling currents as they made progress. They reached the other side of the river and Drustan clambered up the muddy bank and bade his farewell.

"Good luck to you young'un" said the old man and he paddled off to start his delayed fishing.

Chapter 4

Drustan turned again southwards; he didn't know the lie of the land so he tried to avoid the open spaces as much as possible and keep near to the edges of the woods so he could duck in if required. He kept a good lookout and he hid whenever he heard the sounds of approaching people.

He laid up overnight out of sight under the canopy of the trees. He was hungry and tired but was able to drink in the many little streams he came to and crossed. Eventually he joined a large well-used track that seemed to match what the old man had told him about. He had come quite far.

Finally he arrived at a small village and decided it was time to see where he was in the Atrebates' lands. As he moved forwards towards the entrance of the dun a couple of warriors carrying spears came out to confront him.

"I have travelled from far in kinship. Can I speak with your village elder?" he said.

"Why should you wish to speak with him?" said a surly warrior.

"I am come in peace to seek audience with King Verica" replied Drustan.

The other guard murmured something to the first warrior who went back through the entranceway. Several minutes passed by as they stood watching each other and then the other warrior came back and motioned Drustan to follow them inside the village.

They walked past young and old, man and woman, who viewed Drustan dressed as he was in his old, tattered tribal plaid as something beyond their ken.

They escorted him to the largest round hut and the two warriors passed Drustan through the doorway and waited outside.

The village elder was a wizened old man who looked Drustan up and down.

"What do you want coming here? Are you a spy?"

"I am no spy, and I seek passage to see your king and also find my mother's brother among your tribe. Can you send me safely on the way?"

"So you want to see the king then? Well he is hard pressed at the moment for sure by those warring Catuvellauni who attack and ravage our lands."

"I am no friend of those who have taken over my homelands of the Trinovantes."

"Well in that case I will send you on over to the king's royal dun and he can deal with you."

Drustan was taken to Calleva, the tribal centre of the Atrebates, and shown into the presence of the king. Drustan bowed deeply in respect.

"I am King Verica and what is your purpose in coming here before me?" said a wily looking, late middle-aged man dressed in highly coloured clothes and with a heavy gold torc around his neck.

"My name is Drustan of the Trinovantes. I come to offer homage to the king and also my sword; and I seek shelter with my mother's older brother Kenan."

"Na, your uncle was one of my best warriors, but now he is dead, killed by those dread Catuvellauni."

"Oh no!" exclaimed Drustan.

"So why should I accept the offer of help from one of the Trinovantes who are now themselves quite under the control of the Catuvellauni who oppress me and attack my lands?"

"Because I would offer you my aid in fighting and resisting them."

"What use can a mere stripling like you be to me?"

"I have nothing but hatred of their tribe, their king and those accursed sons of his."

"I say again what use are you to me?"

"I can fight and I know the base natures of the sons of King Cunobelin – and in knowing them I know their weaknesses and the ways they can be fought against. I offer my service and I will not let you down. I pledge my honour to you in the fight ahead."

"Well in honour of my former companion I will accept your homage and your sword in my fight to free my lands from those aggressors the Catuvellauni."

So Drustan was accepted into the ranks of the royal warband of the Atrebates which was led by Bericus, the son of King Verica.

Bericus was a well-liked commander of his men; he seemed pleasant and cheerful but he was a tough leader who expected them to follow his orders loyally and without question.

He welcomed Drustan and made him gifts of a shield and a war spear.

"Together we must fight the Catuvellauni and win back the lands they have taken from us. It may take some time but we shall prevail."

"Thank you for the shield and spear. You have my gratitude and my obedience to follow you into battle."

"Now that King Cunobelin's brother Epaticcus is dead I hope to attack soon and drive them back. We will be facing his second son Caratacus now."

"I know Caratacus and I hate him. He attacked and beat me up before and I owe him back. I have made a sacred vow to harry him forever!"

King Verica and his son soon put into action their plans to fight back against Caratacus and Drustan was swiftly involved in the raids of the warbands. They ambushed and attacked outlying groups of the Catuvellauni and gradually their hit and run tactics worked and they recovered some of the territory formerly lost.

But it came at a price and there was much wailing in many village huts with the deaths of brave husbands and young sons.

Drustan learned more about how to fight and with his horse riding skills and bold manner soon became one of the leading warriors in the royal warband. He was repaying his promise to King Verica to be a worthy fighter.

Chapter 5

But trouble was brewing in the royal family of King Cunobelin; the ageing king was being assailed by infighting between his sons. The youngest Adminius claimed that he was being excluded from power and being badly treated by his older brothers. Togodumnus and Caratacus viewed him as a spoiled and selfish younger brother who was always acting impulsively and causing problems. There was no love lost between the brothers.

Adminius was already installed as a proxy king of the Cantiaci, imposed on them down in the South East, and he stirred them up to revolt and raid the lands of the Catuvellauni.

Togodumnus took the warband of the Catuvellauni down into what is now Kent and subdued the Cantiaci. Adminius was ordered to the court of his father to answer for his deeds and accept punishment.

However the arrogant young man refused to come; his brothers demanded their father take action and Cunobelin, with a heavy heart, was forced into banishing Adminius with exile from Britain.

Adminius had to flee to the South coast and seek a ship to take him over to Gaul. Once there he upset the Roman Governor of Gallia Belgica and it was thought best to send him on to Rome and so to be put under the control of Emperor Caligula.

All of this turmoil and the loss of his favoured youngest son hung heavy on King Cunobelin and plunged him into despair.

A few months later he died and Togodumnus and Caratacus split up control of the lands held between them.

Togodumnus ruled the Catuvellauni homeland based in Verlamion and Caratacus overlorded the Trinovantes' lands from Camulodunon. Caratacus also started putting more pressure on King Verica and the Atrebates.

Events moved apace and King Verica's warbands were beaten and overwhelmed in several savage skirmishes. Even worse Bericus was cut down and killed in one of the fights – this shook the king badly. Gradually the land controlled by the Atrebates shrank again and King Verica was being pressed around his tribal centre of Calleva.

Things were bad and Verica had very few options left. He could put his remaining warriors together and try his hand in one last battle; but some of his followers were muttering that things had gone too far already and that the Catuvellauni forces under Caratacus were too many and too strong.

Or the other course of action was to get out and run away and that is what King Verica decided to do. He gathered together his wife and daughters and those of his closest followers who would come. They took the tribal gold in coins and jewellery and started to head out on horses and in several carts towards the nearest harbour.

King Verica came up to Drustan and told him to join them.

"You must come with us as you are no friend of the Catuvellauni" said the much older looking king.

"I would rather stay and fight Caratacus" replied Drustan.

"Na, there is no good will come of that; you will just be killed for no honour. Come with us and there may be a chance for revenge and retribution in the future."

So Drustan picked up his sword and belongings and got on a pony to follow them.

When they reached the South coast King Verica used some of his gold to buy them passage on a large trading ship sailing over to the port of Gesoriacum in northern Gallia Belgica.

As they crossed the sea between Britain and Gaul Drustan wondered when he would next see his homeland, or if ever again now that he was an exile.

Chapter 6

When they reached Gesoriacum King Verica was greeted by Roman soldiers who directed that he would be taken to see the Roman Governor over in Durocortorum.

All of the Atrebates plus Drustan were escorted over the next few days by a cohort of auxiliaries travelling on straight built Roman roads to the provincial capital of Gallia Belgica.

At the army fort in the centre of Durocortorum King Verica was shown into the Governor's quarters. The Governor was not overjoyed to see yet another Briton tribal king on the run in exile arriving in his territory to be dealt with.

He was just considering what to say when King Verica spoke.

"I have no wish to be a burden to you. I desire to go to Rome to prostrate myself before the Emperor and ask him to provide soldiers for me to re-conquer my lands and also Britain for the glory and honour of Rome."

Well the Governor was most pleased by this turn of events that he could now pass this king and his followers on down the line to Rome. Let the Emperor deal with more of these puffed-up, petty little kings he thought to himself.

When King Verica told his people that they would be going onto Rome to see the Emperor his daughters were most excited and clapped their hands together.

But Drustan was not so pleased; he did not want to keep travelling and go all that way to Rome. He wanted to stay near to Britain so that one day he might go back.

Anyway he spoke to the king, "I am sorry but I do not want to go to Rome. I will stay here – I do not know what I will do but perhaps I can get a place with the Roman soldiers, maybe working with the horses."

"If you wish it then so be it" said King Verica. "You have fought for me well and done your duty. Maybe we shall meet again some day."

"I thank you for my place with your warriors and the honour I have earned" replied Drustan and he gave his leave to King Verica and walked away from the other Britons.

Chapter 7

Yet what exactly was he to do? He walked out into the large fort and looked around; over at the far end of the complex was a parade ground and his eyes were drawn to some wooden fenced corrals with horses in them.

Drustan wandered over towards one of the corrals where a small group of soldiers were standing around surveying one of their number who was getting ready to try and ride one of the young, unbroken horses therein.

"Come on Frontinus, what are you waiting for?" said a short man with wiry brown hair.

"For you to shut up for once" said the other who must be Frontinus, a big and bearded giant of a man.

"Well that'll never happen" responded a round-faced man with bowed legs and a ready smile.

"Ten sesterces says you can't stay on that horse for more than ten heartbeats" shouted out a fourth soldier with red hair leaning against the fence.

"You're on Galbus, I'll take that bet and be drinking fine wine tonight on your pay" said Frontinus.

He clambered over the fence and approached the chestnut horse fretting nearby; he threw a rope halter over its head and grabbing part of the mane he tried to jump aboard. The horse skittered and then jerked away leaving Frontinus grasping at thin air and he came down heavily on his bottom with a loud thump in the churned up sand and dirt.

He got up ruefully and dusted himself down and advanced again on the wild-eyed beast. He grappled with the rope but the horse pulled away again and dragged the Roman along after him. Things were not going well and the more

Frontinus tried to pull the horse towards him the more the frightened animal shied away.

Catcalls rang out from several of his fellow soldiers.

"Said you couldn't ride that one."

"Oh shut up, fat lot of help you are" said Frontinus, who then glared over at Drustan who was looking on. "What are you doing there, boy, with your mouth hanging open, eh?"

"Well I was just watching you make a mess of training that animal" cracked back Drustan, perhaps rather foolishly.

"Oh, if you can do any better then I'd like to see that, you young pup" shouted Frontinus angrily.

"Now that's not very pleasant of you Frontinus" said the short man.

"I don't feel 'very pleasant' right now if you don't mind" snapped Frontinus as he threw the rope down and backed away from the horse.

"Let me have a try to ride him then" said Drustan who climbed lightly over the fence and stood beside the big Roman.

The youth had always been good with horses and seemed to have a way to coax and quiet them. He calmly advanced and with soothing words learnt from his forefathers moved closer.

The horse looked at him with wide eyes and pulled away again but Drustan kept crooning and clicking his tongue and gradually the chestnut calmed down and allowed Drustan to come forward and gently pat him.

He kept talking and stroking the animal for several minutes and then lightly put the rope halter back over its neck. Still stroking him Drustan smoothly mounted the horse and patted his neck and spoke softly into its ears.

The horse shied slightly but in response to his words and attentions seemed to quieten and allow Drustan to walk him around the corral and then slowly trot.

The four Roman soldiers looked on in admiration.

"Well I never" said one in surprise.

Chapter 8

"You seem to know how to handle horses well" grudgingly admitted Frontinus.

"Yes, I had the knowledge of looking after them back home" replied Drustan.

"And where would that be then?" said the red-haired man.

"I come from Britain over the sea" Drustan explained.

"Ah, you have come over with that king from the Atrebates" stated the short man.

"Yes, but I am not with him and not of the Atrebates. My name is Drustan and I am from the Trinovantes tribe."

"I am Frontinus and leader of these men."

"Or so he thinks and I am Marcus" exclaimed the round-faced man. "We are cavalrymen attached to the legion based here, the Legio XX Valeria Victrix."

"Oh don't wind old Frontinus up! I am Galbus from Southern Gaul where the sun always shines unlike here" said the red-haired soldier.

"Don't leave me out then for I am Didius" rejoined the short man with the wiry brown hair.

"So introductions have been made. Now what are you doing here then?" asked Frontinus.

Drustan looked at the four and replied "I don't rightly know what I am going to do here. I had to leave my home over in Britain and I got passage with King Verica, but I am not going away with his group to Rome. I am adrift and just saw the horses and seeing them reminded me of home and past times."

"Maybe you could help out here looking after them?" said Marcus all friendly like, "we are short of stableboys."

"Stablelad, he looks like more of a young warrior to me" said Frontinus, "but some extra help would be useful since we have lost a few to the sweating sickness."

"I would be glad to do something and would appreciate anything useful that will help to keep my belly full and my mind occupied. So that would suit me" said Drustan.

"Let us see what the troop commander says then, but first let us go to the nearest tavern to slake our thirst as I am quite parched with all this dust. Come along with us boy" boomed Frontinus and they walked away from the horses and the corral towards the main gate out of the fort.

"I'm afraid I have no money to pay for drinks" admitted Drustan.

"Don't worry about that! The drinks are on us for showing us some good horse riding skills and trouncing old Frontinus here" said Galbus.

"Watch it - and if you're so flush you can pay" growled the big man.

They soon found a bustling little tavern and sat down at a long table to one side in the crowded, noisy room.

"A jug of wine and five mugs for us, mine host" shouted Frontinus who was definitely leader of the pack.

Drink came and they set to with a vengeance. It was nice for Drustan to feel again in friendly company – something he had not felt for a long time. The soldiers were loud and jovial, always ribbing each other and seemed inclined to include Drustan in their warm and friendly companionship.

"You had best be polite to the troop commander when you speak to him. He is proud of the reputation of his turma of cavalry."

"Dracus is a hard man but fair, so he might be amenable to taking you on. But watch out because he is a stickler for rules and orders."

"Always banging on about training and formations, and on and on" hiccupped a slightly inebriated and now red-faced Marcus.

"I will do my best" said Drustan who also was somewhat affected by the wine, which he was not that well accustomed to.

"So what do you think of this fine wine then?"

"More like the bottom of the barrel to me!" said Galbus, perhaps a little bit too loudly.

The innkeeper scowled over at them.

"I am more used to mead than wine" replied Drustan.

Chapter 9

Eventually they spilled out onto the street and headed back towards the Roman fort. Sobering up quickly in the cool evening air, they walked in through the main gate and went over towards an annexe of the headquarters building. The four cavalrymen led Drustan to a small room and knocked on the door frame and then stood to attention.

"What is it now?" said a tall swarthy man with short black hair greying at the temples.

"Decurion Dracus, we come with a possible replacement for the troop" said Frontinus pushing Drustan forward.

"What by Hades, this young pup?" exclaimed Dracus.

"He is a good horseman" interjected Didius.

"Well if you say so then he must be!" sarcastically said the Decurion.

"Oh no, he really is – he quietened that young chestnut stallion that Frontinus couldn't seem to ride" said Marcus.

"Well that doesn't surprise me either then!"

"My name is Drustan and know that I rode in a king's warband and fought long and hard in his service" interrupted Drustan, whose cheeks were growing redder and whose temper, perhaps due to the effects of the wine, was slightly rising.

"He is a good lad in need of employment and could make himself useful" explained Galbus.

"What, you expect me to take on all your drinking cronies, eh?" shouted Dracus, but there was a slight twinkle in his eyes.

"I will not beg for a place if you do not want me" replied Drustan.

"Steady on lad" said Frontinus.

"Nay, nay, Drustan, maybe we can use you. Perhaps we can take you on as a stableboy and see how things go."

"Surely we could take him into the troop?" said Marcus.

"I said we will see how things go" said Dracus. "Now take him over to the stables and hand him over to the head stableman of our horses to deal with."

So Drustan started out working in the cavalry stables. Now the grey-haired old trooper who was the head stableman was quite suspicious and severe to start with, but once he saw how good with horses Drustan was he soon warmed to him.

Every day Dracus' troop came over to pick up their mounts and go over to the large parade ground to do drills and try out their horses in formations.

Drustan observed the training and thought it something he would be able to do.

He often chatted with his friends, the four cavalrymen, and when they were allowed leave from their posts they were able to go into the town and drink wine in a couple of the local taverns.

Gradually life slipped into a pattern of hard but rewarding work. Then on another day of training, one of the troop's other cavalrymen, in attempting a jump over a wooden hurdle, fell awkwardly and broke his leg badly.

The legion was due to go out on important manoeuvres the next day in front of the Legate and this would leave the troop one man short.

Dracus then came over to Drustan who was with his friends.

"Looks like we are a man down so perhaps you could join the troop for our exercises and I can see what you are made of. Mind you best be careful and stay out of trouble!"

"Oh thank you and I will not let you down" said Drustan.

"Well just stay on your horse and follow what these four others do and don't step out of line" replied Dracus.

And Drustan did as he was told and stuck close to his four fellow companions. The legion marched out and went around the local region to make the Gallic tribes aware of its presence and show its power.

The cavalry had a scouting function and all of the four turmae were always moving ahead and to the sides keeping watch.

When they got back to the fort at Durocortorum Dracus pulled him to one side and said to Drustan "I believe you have done quite well – you will need more training, but I think there is a place in the troop for you, so come and sign up and join if you want."

"Yes I would like that" replied Drustan.

And so he was warmly accepted into the troop and especially by his four friends who kept an eye on him as he trained with them.

The days turned cold and winter set in; heavy snow stopped them patrolling outside the town and all the soldiers and their horses felt cooped up. Occasionally tempers frayed and a few fist fights occurred.

However eventually temperatures rose and a thaw took place, and then the muddy roads dried out as spring came again.

Chapter 10

News came from the port of Gesoriacum of further unrest and trouble over in Britain. The brothers Togodumnus and Caratacus were extending their power further in the South East. No other tribes could stand against them and their behaviour and lack of respect for Rome and the Emperor irked and worried the Roman generals over in Gaul.

Then suddenly they all heard that Emperor Caligula had been killed and the Praetorian Guard had named his uncle Claudius as the new Emperor.

Although previously thought of as underwhelming and insignificant, Emperor Claudius turned out to be a shrewd and clever new ruler. He realised that to look good to the Roman Senate and the people it would be sensible to expand the scope and size of the Empire.

That is where the previous appeal of King Verica for assistance in regaining his throne came in useful. The unrest and warring tribes made Britain an attractive target for Roman expansion; along with the lure of its wealth in minerals, gold and also slaves.

So Emperor Claudius decided to send his general Aulus Plautius with four legions over to Britain to subdue and conquer it for Rome.

The legions were assembled and marched to Gesoriacum and preparations were made to take ship across the Oceanus Britannicus.

For many an ordinary soldier the impending invasion would have meant the certainty of hard fighting along with the then tantalising prospect of looting and booty.

But Britain was just then still thought of as an island at the end of the known world filled with Druids and strange painted warriors and customs, and many of the Roman soldiers would have been scared about the whole venture.

In fact some of the soldiers refused to set foot on the ships at first, but the Emperor sent a freedman called Narcissus to address them.

The sending of an ex-slave was deemed such an insult that to avoid further humiliation the soldiers backed down and finally obeyed the orders to board ship.

Our cavalrymen embarked as well with their horses being placed into wooden stalls down in the hold. The comrades were a combination of excited, tense and fatigued.

When they had set sail the wind got up and the sea turned rough; surprisingly the giant Frontinus rushed over to the side and proceeded to be seasick.

"I never thought you would have such a precious stomach" said Marcus.

"Oh, but the whole deck seems to be moving; and the sky rolling around – just you wait!" groaned Frontinus.

And shortly thereafter he was joined at the ship side by Marcus and Didius retching away.

Galbus looked over at Drustan who like him seemed fine, "Doesn't bother me, when I was younger I used to go out to sea fishing with my father and brothers long before I joined up!" he chortled.

"Come on you lily-livered landlubbers" shouted over Dracus "and stop puking and go below and see to the horses."

So they held it in and went below into the cramped confines of the hold; but at least having something to do took their minds off their poorly stomachs and gradually they got more used to the roll of the ship and the swell of the sea.

With the horses quieted and seen to they came back up on deck; ahead they could see some white cliffs which soon loomed larger and nearer.

"Nearly there now lads" said Dracus suddenly appearing at their sides, "just got to find somewhere to anchor and then we'll make landfall."

Later on that afternoon the fleet of ships found a decent anchorage and a long shingle beach on which to land on.

There were a few Briton horsemen seen on the horizon but they made no movements to disrupt the landing and after a bit they just moved off.

The soldiers disembarked and the horses and all necessary supplies were unloaded. Next the army moved slightly inland away from the beach and encamped for the night.

It felt a bit strange for Drustan to be back in his old homeland.

Chapter 11

The next day the legions advanced further inland and the cavalry units scouted ahead and came in contact with the Britons.

Dracus led his troop on nearer and then they looked on as the enemy retreated into nearby woodland to try and avoid a pitched battle.

However Aulus Plautius was keen to give battle and sent forward some auxiliary troops to push into the fringes of the trees and drive them out.

The tribesmen were forced out and after a brief skirmish had to flee to get away from the legions.

But the Britons had been defeated and the prestige of the Catuvellauni and their leaders Togodumnus and Caratacus had been damaged in the eyes of the other tribes.

The Romans now showed their expertise in campaigning and engineering by quickly constructing a large wooden fort with earthen ditches around it in which the legions made camp.

Having escaped across the river Medway the Britons thought they were safe from attack, but an auxiliary unit and some of the cavalry forded the river and took the tribesmen by surprise killing many of their horses in the process.

Then General Vespasian led some units of his Legio II Augusta across the river to kill the stranded Britons. However the fighting was fierce and evenly matched. This time the tribes did not flee but held on till night fell and subsequently the battle continued the next day.

The commander of Legio IX Hispana was Gnaeus Hosidius Geta and in the attack he was almost captured. But Dracus' cavalry turma came to his aid and Frontinus and his companions cleaved a way through to his side.

Drustan speared a native warrior who had just hacked down the standard bearer and he picked up the Eagle standard and held it aloft.

Seeing this Gnaeus Hosidius Geta then rallied his troops and turned the battle so decisively in the favour of the Romans that later on he was awarded a 'Roman Triumph' along with all its trophies.

The Britons finally fell back and managed to cross over the next river Tamesis. Once again auxiliary cavalry forded the river and attacked the tribes being led by Togodumnus and Caratacus.

Meanwhile upstream Roman military engineers had put together a pontoon bridge made up of wooden sections laid on top of boats and rafts.

The bulk of the Roman army now crossed over and piled into the flank of the Britons. The fighting was ferocious and into the thickest part was flung the Legio XX and Dracus' cavalry troop.

Galbus was knocked off his horse and hewn down by the wild warriors fighting there.

Frontinus, Didius and Marcus charged on their horses and were able to drag back his shattered body.

Galbus managed to speak one last time: "At least I shall die with my friends around me."

Sadly they laid him down at the rear with other Roman casualties and then went back to the battle.

Drustan was ahead of them, fighting wildly. They joined him and fought on side by side. Then Drustan spotted a war chieftain he recognised – it was Togodumnus who was leading a group of Catuvellauni warriors around to the rear of the Roman force.

Shouting out a warning to Dracus, Drustan and the others wheeled their horses round to face this new threat and charged.

They smashed into this group like a wave crashing onto the shore – slashing swords and thrusting spears were breaking up this enemy formation.

Suddenly Drustan came across Togodumnus and they fought; fuelled with anger Drustan slashed and parried the other man's thrusts.

His opponent was older and more experienced but Drustan managed to get control of his rage and channel it. He pushed Togodumnus back and then his adversary slipped on the bloody ground and Drustan was able to bring his sword down crushingly into the other's chest and finish him off.

The eyes of the great chieftain dimmed and his life blood ran out – the old enemy of Drustan's youth was dead.

At the sight of the fall of their king the Britons broke and ran; many of their number were hacked down in the pursuit by the Roman army. The rout carried on till the fading of the daylight and many were left dead as they tried to flee back into their Catuvellauni homelands.

Chapter 12

Next Aulus Plautius halted the advance with the Southern tribes defeated; and with their eventual success now certain, he sent word for Emperor Claudius to join the army for the final push and ultimate victory.

Drustan and his friends now mourned the loss of Galbus – it was a heavy blow and the bitter taste took away the thrill of victory.

Dracus came and found Drustan, "It is sad to lose a close comrade like Galbus, but you have done well in these battles. Without your warning maybe that chieftain Togodumnus would have got behind us and turned the course of the fight."

"His loss wipes out all the honour I have gained" muttered Drustan sadly.

"No, not all your brave deeds can be forgotten. I have heard rumours that Gnaeus Hosidius Geta wishes to have you rewarded for your saving of the Eagle standard of Legio IX Hispana back there."

The Emperor Claudius duly arrived shortly thereafter bringing with him some strange beasts called elephants, fresh troops and also a squad of shiny gold armoured Praetorian Guards as his bodyguards.

The Southern tribes that had formally been under the control of the Catuvellauni came to surrender and offer supplication to the Roman Emperor.

The Roman legions marched on the Catuvellauni capital of Camulodunon and occupied it and swiftly built a military fort there.

Emperor Claudius was most happy at the extent of all his glorious triumph!

He was also there at the formal commemoration when Gnaeus Hosidius Geta presented Drustan with a fantastically decorated Roman cavalry ceremonial helmet that was made of silver-gilded iron and embellished in places with thick gold leaf.

It came with not two but with six detachable cheekpieces depicting scenes from history and mythology, including one showing a Roman Emperor being crowned by the goddess Victory whilst trampling a barbarian under his horse's hooves.

The Emperor graciously added a large bag of coins to the honours given to Drustan.

After the ceremony his friends gathered round him and Frontinus slapped him on the back.

"Well done youngster, you bring great honour to the legion."

"And to be presented to the Emperor like that is most rare" said Marcus. "Let's see that helmet up close; my, how it shines in the sunlight."

"No, let us feel the weight of that big bag of coins" chortled Didius.

It certainly was a fabulous gift that Drustan later wore at various parades. It certainly marked him out for his valour.

Chapter 13

So Emperor Claudius had his great triumph to celebrate and went back to Rome and held a grand victory parade there.

Yet however the real remaining issue was that the Catuvellauni weren't totally defeated just yet. Caratacus had retreated over to the West where he re-emerged in alliance with the tribes of South Wales such as the Silures, and he caused further trouble along with them and the Druids.

Thus the Romans were set for a longer war as they sought to extend their power over further parts of Britain and also had to deal with Caratacus' continuing guerrilla fighting.

The legions carried on fighting skirmishes, but there were no more pitched battles and gradually the Romans gained control over more tribes including the Iceni in the East and the Brigantes in the North.

The Legio XX Valeria Victrix was stationed in Camulodunon, soon to be renamed Camulodunum, and when things were a bit more settled and they were finally given a spell of leave Drustan set out for his old tribe of the Trinovantes.

He rode through Verlamion, which was now garrisoned with Roman soldiers, and then onto his old home to see his mother and also because he was looking for Silla – after all these years he still wanted to see her and find out how things had gone with her after he had to run away.

When he appeared in the village dressed as a Roman cavalryman there were some suspicious looks and guarded expressions.

He asked to see the elders of the village, but there were none the same that he remembered from past times. Then one younger man stepped out and came forward who Drustan recognised.

"Aiee, Drustan, so you still live and are now a Roman soldier I see."

"Yes, I have returned and I see things are much changed here. And how is my dear mother?"

"Oh yes, they surely have changed. Alas sadly your mother died last year, they say of a broken heart. After you went the Catuvellauni lorded it over us and got rid of many of the old elders. Now we are under the rule of the Romans but it is not much different than being under the yoke of the Catuvellauni. At least we have heard that Togodumnus is dead."

"Yes, I killed him" said Drustan.

The men of the Trinovantes murmured amongst themselves and stared at Drustan with something between vague admiration and veiled hostility.

"So what else have you come back for?" enquired the younger man.

"I have also come to seek news of the girl Silla."

"Na, because of your fight with Adminius and his brothers, and because of her being in disgrace, Silla was cast out and sent away to live with the Corieltauvi."

"The disgrace was not hers – she was being attacked and I fought to save both her life and her honour."

"Things went hard with us because of your actions" said one of the older men. "The Catuvellauni cowed us and took reprisals. The girl had to go for her own sake and for ours."

"As far as we know she is still up North" said the younger man.

"Then I will go and find her" said Drustan and he got back on his horse and left his former home with no real affection remaining and no backward look.

Chapter 14

Drustan headed northwards to the heart of Britain and towards the territory of the Corieltauvi and their tribal centre of Ratae.

The Corieltauvi were a largely agricultural people who had few strongly defended sites and they had offered little or no resistance to Roman rule.

When he reached Ratae Drustan went to see the tribal leader (now essentially a sub-king under the control of the Romans) and enquired about the whereabouts of Silla.

Apparently she had not got on with the other women of the royal dun and had been sent away again to a smaller village over to the East. Drustan remounted his horse and turned away from the setting sun and rode on.

Later on just before night was falling Drustan arrived at a small, dirty little village. The dull-eyed villagers stared at him with deep suspicion as strangers were unusual and mostly unwelcome.

One cloaked woman walking back into the village with a bucket of water turned and looked directly at him and suddenly with a cry dropped the bucket. It was Silla, but not quite as young and fresh-looking as he remembered.

"Drustan is it really you?" exclaimed the woman.

"Aiee, it is me. I have come back to find you."

"Oh my, by the gods, you are a sight to see."

"And so are you. I have waited years for this day and to see you again."

"It has been so long; I thought you were dead."

"I have been close to death at times but not taken yet. How are you faring, dearest Silla?"

"Things have not gone well since we parted. I was sent away and have ended up here as a sort of servant to the village elder and his wife. A difficult couple who make me work harder than is right."

"I am sorry that I had to leave you like that but it seemed the only thing to do at the time."

"Yes, but if you had returned Togodumnus or Caratacus with their warriors would have surely killed you. I do not blame you for leaving, but my life has gone from bad to worse. I cannot believe how things have turned out. Now I am tired out and worn down."

"You still look lovely to me" shyly muttered Drustan.

"Oh, you think by flattering me you can get straight back into my affections" laughed Silla.

"I would hope to win my way back into your good graces" said Drustan as he bowed towards her.

Then coming out of a hut an old man with a stick moved towards them.

He said brusquely to Silla "What is going on? Who is this man here?"

She replied "He is an old friend from my tribe come to find me."

"Well that's nothing to do with me and your duties that are owed to us. Get back to work now."

"Not so fast" interrupted Drustan "this woman is a good friend of mine and I will not see her disrespected so badly. I am a soldier of Rome with battle honours and I command you to treat her properly."

"Why should I listen to you, eh!" stormed the village elder.

Silla looked cowed and crestfallen.

"Because I have a sword to uphold my rights and a right arm to enforce my wishes. Yet I am a reasonable man; I have coins that I will give to you to enable this woman to live as a freewoman here with servants of her own."

Silla looked brighter and smiled over at Drustan.

"Well in that case maybe we can reach an understanding then."

"I certainly hope so – especially for your sake!"

And so a deal was brokered and money changed hands and the whole matter was sorted out. Silla could stay there in the village as a freewoman by rights with her own hut and a young girl to assist and serve her.

Silla and Drustan talked further together and discussed what the future might hold. So much had happened and it would take time for them to get accustomed to one another again.

Drustan had to go back to his service in the Roman army but promised to come back and see her whenever he could.

For her part Silla said she still cared for him and would stay there and await his returns.

The next day Drustan reminded the village elder to keep his promises and take care that Silla was kept safe and left alone.

Drustan kissed Silla goodbye and she waved as he rode off to report back to the legion.

Chapter 15

And so Drustan returned to the ranks of the Legio XX Valeria Victrix and his companions in the cavalry turma.

The Romans continued to expand their sphere of influence over the surrounding tribes and lands. There was sporadic fighting here and there but the power of the Roman legions was too much for the brave but ill-organised tribesmen to resist.

However Caratacus was still a problem – he was always out there stirring up trouble and there were often hit and run raids made by his remaining loyal Catuvellauni and his co-conspirators the Silures.

Yet he did not manage to inspire vast numbers of the Britons into a mass revolt which would have really troubled the growing Roman presence.

Military life dragged on for Drustan and he was able to visit Silla several times, passing through the growing town of Ratae.

Her status in the village was now secure and she always seemed to be pleased to see him. For his part Drustan sensed a re-kindling of the love he had always felt for Silla.

But Roman soldiers could not wed their women when they were still in the ranks; and a woman could only be near them by being camp followers or living in tents or shacks outside the walls of Roman forts.

This was something neither Silla or Drustan were wanting to happen in their case. They cared deeply for each other and wanted somehow to make it work.

Later however one autumn time Drustan came to visit Silla but he could not find her at her hut nor could he see her young servant girl.

Drustan went to find the village elder.

"What is going on? Where is Silla?"

"Aiee, it is so sad! She was with child and she died giving birth. You have a little baby daughter who is being looked after by that young servant girl and her mother."

"Oh no! No!" exclaimed Drustan – he was totally shocked – how could this be! He had not even known that Silla was with child.

"We have not had chance to reach you to send word of this tragedy."

Drustan was completely shattered – somehow he had thought the rest of his life would be bound up with Silla and now she was gone.

But he went to see the young girl who was looking after his baby daughter.

"Silla held the baby and named her Breaca before she died. I and my mother can continue to look after her if you want us to."

Drustan agreed this was best and gave her a small bag of coins to use to take care of herself and the baby.

He also spoke to the village elder to make sure he would keep an eye out for them.

Chapter 16

Sorrowfully Drustan went back to Camulodunon where the Legio XX was stationed and tried to get back into the routines of military life, but he found it oh so hard. He spoke to his friends and told them what had happened and they tried to console him.

Eventually the legion moved out of Camulodunon to a new fort in Gloucester further West, and a colony of veterans and ex-soldiers was established at the newly re-named town of Colonia Camulodunum.

The legions still continued to go after Caratacus and finally the next year the recently arrived Governor Publius Ostorius Scapula led the Legio IX and the Legio XX into a big battle against Caratacus and his allies, the Silures and the Ordovices tribes.

Caratacus chose a battlefield in hilly country, placing the Britons on the higher ground and this position made any approach difficult for the Romans. Where the slope was shallow, he ordered built rough stone ramparts and placed armed men behind them.

The Roman commander, Publius Ostorius Scapula, was reluctant to assault the opposing lines, but the enthusiasm of his men won him over.

The river was crossed more easily than expected, but the Roman soldiers came under a heavy fire of missiles and they employed the testudo formation to protect themselves and move forward and pull apart the stone ramparts.

Once into the inner defences the Romans broke through and bloody hand-to-hand fighting commenced. The Britons broke and ran, but they were caught between the legionaries and the auxiliary cavalry and decimated.

After all this time chasing and fighting Caratacus it was good to see him finally utterly defeated. Though Caratacus' wife, son and daughter were captured, Caratacus himself escaped – but only for a short time.

He fled North seeking refuge among the Brigantes tribe, but their Queen Cartimandua, wishing to show her loyalty, handed him over in chains to the Romans.

Historical Footnote:

Ultimately Caratacus was sent over to Rome for execution and exhibited in chains as part of the Emperor Claudius' Roman Triumph. However Caratacus acted bravely and gave such a good speech in front of the Roman Senate that the Emperor decided to spare him and his family and also gave him an imperial pension to live on.

Chapter 17

What to do now that Caratacus had been defeated?

Frontinus, Didius and Marcus had all by now done enough years of military service so that they could retire and leave the legions.

So the three decided to take the pensions and land grants offered and retire back to the colonia of veterans at Camulodunum where they had been stationed so often before.

They swiftly took wives and settled down as farmers and merchants and soon became prominent members of town society.

But Drustan had to stay on in the legions; however it was decided that due to his meritorious service he would be specially promoted to the post of Decurion in an auxiliary cavalry unit to be transferred overseas.

Before he left Britain he said goodbye to his longstanding friends who wished him all the best for his future campaigns.

Also Drustan ventured one last time to the little Corieltauvi village and left more money with the girl there, and also some with the village elder who he had grown to like and trust more.

On that final night there he went outside the village, and in a clump of trees on a windy hilltop by the side of an earthen circle that was a shrine of the Corieltauvi, he buried the ceremonial helmet and other goods in what he considered a place of safety in these uncertain times before his forthcoming travels.

The next day he bade a fond farewell to the young child that was his daughter Breaca and headed off on his travels.

Chapter 18

The young and infamous Nero was now the Emperor as for many more years Drustan fought overseas in various campaigns of the Roman Empire – some in the desert regions of Northern Africa and also in other strange but exotic lands of the Eastern provinces.

He commanded many different men and lost quite a few over the years – that was never an easy thing to deal with.

Also over time Drustan picked up a few wounds and eventually it was decided that he should be invalided out of the legions with a full pension.

But when he arrived back in Southern Britain things were not as quiet as he might have expected after all these further years.

The tribes were still just as fractious and more trouble was brewing – some of it partly fuelled by the heavy-handed actions of some of the more unscrupulous Roman officials running the province, often seemingly for their own personal financial benefit.

He passed through Calleva and heard further rumours that there was serious unrest boiling up in the lands of the Iceni.

Now the cause of the growing disturbance was overbearing and harsh mistreatment by the most oppressive and arrogant Romans.

The Iceni King Prasutagus (long celebrated for his prosperity) had died and in his will had named the Emperor joint heir along with his own two daughters; an act of deference which he thought would place his kingdom and household beyond the risk of injury and disinheritance.

The result was just the opposite – so much so that his late kingdom and household were pillaged by the greedy, avaricious Roman agents as though they had been prizes of war.

Furthermore his widow Boudica was savagely whipped and his two daughters were viciously assaulted, and also the estates of the leading Iceni men were confiscated and seized.

This was a truly shocking situation ready to explode into further violence.

And just then the current Roman Governor, Gaius Suetonius Paulinus, was far away engaged in a campaign against the stronghold of the Druids on the distant island of Mona.

Chapter 19

Drustan decided to ride on to the North and that little village of the Corieltauvi where his daughter hopefully still lived.

What would she look like now he wondered? Surely she would be almost a young woman by now?

When he passed through Ratae he could sense the growing unease. He reached the village and was welcomed by the village elder – now grown quite an old man.

"Sa, it is good to see you after all these years away."

"It is good to be back too. How is my daughter?"

"Ah, she has grown up to be a fine young woman. Come and see."

So they went and he greeted his long unseen daughter again. It was strange but she looked so like her mother that Drustan felt a sudden pang in the depths of his heart.

Breaca was nearly fifteen years old now and soon would be old enough to marry. It seemed she had quite a few admirers in the dun but there was one young, tall lad who she seemed to favour most with her smiles.

And it occurred to Drustan looking on that he could be quite a good sort of man to look after and take care of Breaca.

Later on he spoke with the village elder who said that was his own nephew and confirmed he would see that things were dealt with appropriately in the future.

Thus with matters seemingly settled for his daughter's future in the village Drustan considered what to do next.

Then suddenly a rider came in from the direction of Ratae with terrible news – Queen Boudica and the whole of the Iceni tribe had risen in revolt and were up in arms and aiming to destroy all traces of Roman rule in Britain.

Drustan told the villagers to stay put and steer clear of getting caught up in the revolt, which he said would surely ultimately not succeed.

He said goodbye once more to his daughter Breaca and wished her salutations for the future.

"By being away so much, I know it seems like I have ignored you, but know that I and your mother have always loved you."

He thought it best to leave his Roman helmet and ceremonial goods still buried out there in the trees.

He decided to go join his old friends in the colonia established at Camulodunum. If he had to get involved in the fighting he would rather it be by the side of his former comrades.

He hurriedly rode cross-country South East towards Camulodunum.

Chapter 20

All this while the Iceni had gathered strength from other tribes including the Trinovantes, who felt as badly treated by the Romans as they had been by the Catuvellauni.

Especially because when the Roman veterans had set up the colonia in Camulodunum they had mistreated and displaced many of the Trinovantes people, and also built a grand temple to the former Emperor Claudius at great local expense, making the town a target for much native resentment.

Queen Boudica was an imposing figure; she was tall with tawny hair hanging down to below her waist, with a harsh voice and a piercing gaze.

Boudica addressed and inspired her army with these words:

"It is not as a woman descended from noble ancestry, but as one of the people that I am avenging lost freedom, my scourged body and the outraged chastity of my daughters."

All the people in the assembled crowd shouted and roared their approval.

"Death to the Romans and freedom once more for the tribes of Britain" yelled out the queen.

Chapter 21

Drustan rode into Colonia Camulodunum. All was in uproar and chaos – frightened people were rushing about everywhere. He moved forwards into the town where he could see barricades being put up across the roads to block access to the centre.

Then he saw men he formerly knew from the legions including his old friends.

"What are you doing here, old comrade?" shouted Frontinus, now with a grey beard and thinning hair.

"I thought you could maybe do with some help" said Drustan.

"Well maybe you might be getting more than you bargained for" called out Didius.

"I like a good fight."

"This may end up being more than that" exclaimed Marcus.

They embraced once more as friends. They were all older and good living had put weight on the veteran soldiers.

"How go things with you?" said Frontinus.

"I was invalided out of the legions and came back to Britain looking for some peace and quiet!"

"Looks like you got that wrong then" chuckled Didius.

"Seems so."

"Have you seen your daughter? Is she well?" enquired Marcus.

"Yes, I have seen her and she is all grown up. I have told her to stay safe in that out of the way village of hers."

Drustan then asked "Have messengers been sent out requesting help?"

"Ah, now that's a slight problem there" explained Frontinus. "You see most of the legions are away over in the far North West fighting the damn Druids. So the Governor isn't fully in control of the whole situation. It's a mess."

Didius added "The Procurator in Londinium, Catus Decianus, was asked for help and yet has only sent just two hundred auxiliary troops."

"Well what preparations are being made for defence?"

"We are digging ditches and raising obstacles around the centre of the town to form rough fortifications."

"The women and children are being brought into the forum area, by the side of the Temple to the Divine Claudius."

"That temple caused a lot of trouble between us and the local tribes you know!" said Marcus.

"We will make the best preparations we can" replied Frontinus, "but things will certainly be tough. We hope we can hold out till more reinforcements come."

"Suetonius should surely be on his way back with the legions by now?" Didius wondered aloud.

"I certainly hope so!" and Marcus raised his eyes to the heavens.

They carried on working on strengthening the barricades.

Later on as twilight faded they went back into the centre of the colonia. Drustan saw their wives and young children – his heart sank as realised all that his friends had to lose. The situation was gut-wrenchingly awful but like them he tried to keep a straight face and appear calm and not panicked.

Nightime was hardly quiet with all the bustle and noise of the frightened families and crying, upset children.

In a slightly quieter corner round the back of the temple precinct Drustan sat and drank from a flask of fine wine.

"I see you have grown to like wine now!"

"Yes Frontinus, I have had long enough to acquire the taste for it" replied Drustan.

"I'm glad that I can catch a word with you on your own now. You know things are not going to go well here?"

"I kind of got that impression."

"You've got a fast horse; you could leave and go now."

"I don't think I would find that right."

"No one would think bad of you. I could say that you have gone to Londinium to try and get more help."

"I have my honour and pride to think of."

"Damn your honour if you're going to end up dead!"

"Well if I am going to die then I'd rather die in battle fighting with my old comrades" declared Drustan.

"So may it be then, Drustan, but I thank you for your help and for being here as a friend" Frontinus quietly said and slapped him on the back and walked away.

Chapter 22

The next day broke cloudy and windless. The Roman defenders stood to arms and manned the rough ramparts and barricades around the colonia centre.

The atmosphere was tense and expectant. The women and children were moved inside the temple for safety.

Then they heard the sounds of tumult growing ever nearer – the tramp of many feet, the clashing of arms, the squeaking of wagon wheels and the clamour of thousands of tribespeople.

Gradually a vast horde appeared in front of them. Boudica stood up in her giant war-chariot with her two daughters riding behind her. She raised her warspear high in the air and a great shout of anger rose from the mass of people.

Native horns harshly blared out. The warriors now ran forward and attacked the defences and the Romans sheltering behind them. The hand-to-hand fighting was vicious with swords hacking and spears thrusting amidst contorted angry faces.

The weight of numbers of the tribesmen broke through the barricades in several places but the gallant defenders threw them back with fanatical bravery and foolhardy sacrifice.

They were sorely pressed but the first assault was repulsed and the tribal warriors fell back to the great multitude waiting beyond.

Drustan checked that his companions were still all right and they saluted each other. They each had a swig of wine from a flask that Didius had brought with him.

"Thirsty work, eh" he grimaced.

"I wonder what they plan to do next?" said Marcus.

They didn't have long to wait as the Britons attacked once again. The brutal combat was fierce and many amongst the veterans and auxiliaries were hewn down and killed.

Gaps were appearing along the barricades and suddenly a group of Iceni broke through and rushed towards Drustan and the others.

They fought stoutly and held them at bay, but then a spear thrust caught Marcus in the chest and he fell down dead – and with that his ready smile was extinguished for ever.

They were being overwhelmed.

"Fall back to the temple!" shouted Frontinus, and as he and Drustan held back the foes Didius dragged Marcus' body away from the fray towards the temple precinct.

They fought outside and more on both sides were killed, but the pressure was telling on the dwindling Romans.

The remaining defenders ran back inside the temple and shut and barred the heavy wooden doors and tried to block up the window holes.

The tribesmen attacked the doors and walls but could not break in though more Romans were killed by missiles thrown in. Didius was hit by a large stone and blood started pouring out of a bad head wound.

The injured were moved to the rear and tended by some of the older women whilst the other mothers tried to soothe their terrified young children.

Chapter 23

Frontinus and Drustan were both exhausted and carrying several wounds; in particular Frontinus had a bad gash on his sword arm which he had roughly tied up as best he could.

From outside the temple they could hear further screams of terror as trapped and injured Romans were put to death.

There were not many uninjured fighters left standing inside the temple now.

"By the gods we have killed many of them, but they are as numerous as ears of corn in an abundant wheatfield" grimly declared Frontinus.

"We have lost many good men" Drustan said.

"And old friends!" replied Frontinus.

"Perhaps we can still hold them at bay" said a nearby old soldier.

Drustan and Frontinus looked at each other knowingly and neither of them really believed that likely.

Nighttime fell and the attacks ceased. They could see firelight shining through the window gaps and hear the tribespeople outside shouting, feasting and drinking.

Water was short and food scarce inside the temple; children slept only fitfully and the adults feared too much to sleep at all and nerves were stretched to breaking point. The wounded moaned grievously and the stench of death pervaded throughout.

Dawn came and with the morning light the Britons roused themselves and came on again. They concentrated on trying to break down the temple doors but the heavy wood with iron strips criss-crossing them held firm.

There was a brief respite but the number of defenders was rapidly decreasing and too many swords were blunted and too many spears broken and useless.

Then they heard a cart being wheeled up and shoved against the doors. Next they saw smoke coming in underneath and heard the crackle of flames burning outside.

"They are setting fire to the doors!" shouted someone.

And they had no water left with which to try and wet the wood or put out the flames.

Frontinus and Drustan exchanged glances.

"This is it then, the final assault" said Drustan.

"If this is the end, then we shall die bravely and go to our gods in honour" replied Frontinus.

Flaming brands of wood were also thrown in through the window holes, and as many fires spread flames leapt up and thick smoke rolled throughout the temple.

Suddenly the doors gave way and a surge of tribesmen burst in through the smoke and flames and lunged at the remaining Romans.

Frontinus screamed in fury and the giant boldly rushed at them killing several before he was struck down.

Drustan shouted out in defiance and was then attacked by a group of warriors; he fought on bravely but was overwhelmed and then a spear thrust caught him and brutally ended his life!

The savage Britons rampaged through the burning temple violently killing every man, woman and child there.

AND THAT MIGHT BE WHY THE HELMET WAS NEVER RETRIEVED AND THE HALLATON HOARD WAS LEFT TO BE FOUND MANY CENTURIES LATER BY A METAL DETECTORIST IN AD2000......

Epilogue on the Boudican Revolt and the Death of Queen Boudica

After burning and razing Camulodunum to the ground, Queen Boudica and the Iceni horde headed South towards Londinium.

The future Governor, Quintus Petillius Cerialis, then commanding the Legio IX Hispana was on his way to relieve the colonia but was too late.

He met up with the rebel forces and suffered an overwhelming defeat; all the foot-soldiers with him were killed and only the commander and some of his cavalry escaped.

When news of the revolt reached the current Governor, Gaius Suetonius Paulinus, he hurried down along Watling Street as fast as he could to Londinium.

Londinium was a relatively new settlement, formed after the conquest of AD43, but it had grown to be a thriving merchant centre on the river Tamesis.

Suetonius considered staying in Londinium and giving battle there but considering his lack of numbers and chastened by Petillius' defeat, he decided to march away and sacrifice the town to try and save the province.

All the tears and weeping of the townspeople could not deter him from giving the signal of departure, although he took with him all of those who could or would be able to march away with the soldiers.

Londinium was abandoned to the rebels, who burnt it down, torturing and killing all those unfortunates who had not been evacuated with Suetonius.

The municipium of Verulamium was next to be destroyed. Tens of thousands of Romans and loyal native Britons had been slaughtered so far in a wanton and terrible blood-lust.

Suetonius regrouped his forces. According to the Roman historian Tacitus, he amassed a force of almost ten thousand men with his own Legio XIV Gemina Martia Victrix, some vexillations of Legio XX Valeria Victrix and any available auxiliaries.

The camp prefect of Legio II Augusta, Poenius Postumus, for uncertain reasons ignored the call to action and they stayed out of harm's way in camp in the South West.

The fourth legion in Britain, Legio IX Hispana, had already been defeated and scattered.

Suetonius made a stand for battle somewhere in the Midlands near the Watling Street road.

The rebels were large in numbers but untrained and ill-armed, and they were encumbered with many wagons containing baggage, loot and their families with them.

A set-piece battle was what the Romans wanted and the heavily armoured Romans cut a swathe through the tribesmen.

Fight turned to flight and it became a rout, but retreat was made difficult by the congested cordon of watching wagons that blocked all avenues of escape.

Now the Roman troops gave no quarter and tens of thousands of warriors, women and families were killed on that dread day of immense slaughter of the Britons.

It is said that in defeat Queen Boudica and her two daughters took poison and died – no bodies were ever found.

The defeat of the rebel horde was utterly decisive for the future of Roman Britain over the next few hundred years.

ALSO BY THIS AUTHOR...

ALL SINS MUST BE PAID FOR

Archaeologists working on the route of the Weymouth Relief Road in Dorset in 2008/2009 discovered a burial pit on Ridgeway Hill containing what turned out to be 54 dismembered skeletons and 51 skulls of Vikings executed by local Saxons.

This novelette seeks to offer a plausible tale of what could have happened at a time of great conflict in England between the Saxons under King Aethelred the Unready and the Danes led by Sweyn Forkbeard around the years AD 1002 to 1014.

It is told through the actions of Rolf, an innocent young boy who stows away on a longship heading across to England. But as the story unfolds, Rolf is drawn into a maelstrom of violence and death, and a burning need for revenge that is so all consuming that it changes him forever. And sometimes a man has to pay a heavy price to atone for all his misdeeds. But is there still a chance for redemption?

£5.99   ISBN: 978-0-9567753-5-1

ALSO BY THIS AUTHOR...

CAST NO SHADOW

Marguerite is a young girl who tragically loses all her family in rebellion and fighting in the Duchy of Gascony in France. Coming over to England in 1252 she becomes known as Margot and gets caught up in fractious strife between the barons and the king.

Along with the swordsman Jean de Savignac and the young pickpocket Tom Buckle, Margot is drawn into a web of intrigue as she plots to get the ultimate revenge she craves for. Whilst barely known to history as Margot the Spy, this spirited and quick-witted young woman has a crucial role to play in the unfolding of the dramatic action of the time.

This short novelette offers up an exciting historical story linked to the personality of Simon de Montfort and events leading up to the Second Barons' War with King Henry III and his son Prince Edward culminating in the decisive Battle of Evesham in 1265.

£5.99   ISBN: 978-0-9567753-6-8

ALSO BY THIS AUTHOR...

AWFUL THE MANY FOUL DEEDS

Rory and his younger sister Eva are orphaned in Ireland and are taken in by the kind Lady Affreca, the wife of the English ruler of much of Ulster, the famed and powerful knight John de Courcy.

But times are changing with the accession of King John, a cruel and vindictive despot who cares nothing for his subjects and the rule of law. His dangerous spitefulness will cause the downfall of many.

This short novelette goes back and forth between Ireland and Wales in the early 1200's as Rory is forced to go on the run to keep one step ahead of royal displeasure. Along the way there are friends and foes to deal with in a search for some peace and safety.

£5.99   ISBN: 978-0-9567753-7-5

David's 30 Favourite Rock & Pop Albums

1964	(01)	The Beatles	A Hard Day's Night
1976	(02)	Be-Bop Deluxe	Sunburst Finish
1971	(03)	Caravan	In The Land Of Grey And Pink
1979	(04)	Ry Cooder	Bop Till You Drop
1991	(05)	Crowded House	Woodface
1972	(06)	Deep Purple	Machine Head
1978	(07)	Dire Straits	Dire Straits
1975	(08)	Eagles	One Of These Nights
1977	(09)	Fleetwood Mac	Rumours
1970	(10)	Free	Fire And Water
1973	(11)	Rory Gallagher	Tattoo
1973	(12)	Genesis	Selling England By The Pound
1968	(13)	Jimi Hendrix	Electric Ladyland
1971	(14)	Led Zeppelin	IV (Four Symbols)
1974	(15)	Little Feat	Feats Don't Fail Me Now
1973	(16)	Lynyrd Skynyrd	Pronounced Leh-nerd Skin-nerd
1973	(17)	Pink Floyd	Dark Side Of The Moon
1975	(18)	Pink Floyd	Wish You Were Here
1972	(19)	Steely Dan	Can't Buy A Thrill
1976	(20)	Steely Dan	The Royal Scam
1976	(21)	Al Stewart	Year Of The Cat
1971	(22)	Rod Stewart	Every Picture Tells A Story
1975	(23)	10CC	How Dare You!
1971	(24)	James Taylor	Mud Slide Slim And The Blue Horizon
1994	(25)	Martin Taylor	Spirit Of Django
2005	(26)	Thunder	The Magnificent Seventh
2001	(27)	Peter White	Glow
1971	(28)	The Who	Who's Next
1972	(29)	Wishbone Ash	Argus
1986	(30)	XTC	Skylarking

David's 20 Favourite Guitarists from his Youth

b.1910	DJANGO REINHARDT	Gypsy Jazz Guitarist
b.1933	JULIAN BREAM	Classical Guitarist and Lutenist
b.1942	JIMI HENDRIX	of JIMI HENDRIX EXPERIENCE
b.1944	JIMMY PAGE	of LED ZEPPELIN
b.1945	RITCHIE BLACKMORE	of DEEP PURPLE and RAINBOW
b.1945	DANNY GATTON	Rockabilly and Redneck Jazz
b.1946	PETER GREEN	of original FLEETWOOD MAC
b.1948	RORY GALLAGHER	Irish Blues Rock Guitarist
b.1948	BILL NELSON	of BE-BOP DELUXE
b.1949	ANDREW LATIMER	of CAMEL
b.1950	ANDY POWELL	of WISHBONE ASH
b.1950	TED TURNER	of WISHBONE ASH
b.1950	PAUL KOSSOFF	of FREE
b.1951	PETER HAYCOCK	of CLIMAX BLUES BAND
b.1951	WALTER TROUT	Blues Rock Guitarist
b.1951	ROBBEN FORD	Blues, Jazz and Rock Guitarist
b.1952	GARY MOORE	Rock and Blues Guitarist
b.1953	LAURIE WISEFIELD	of WISHBONE ASH
b.1954	STEVIE RAY VAUGHAN	"SRV" Blues Rock Guitarist
b.1956	MARTIN TAYLOR	Jazz and Solo Guitarist